Victoria Goes to Brazil

To my dear grandfather, Vovô Luís, for the love, respect,
honesty and dignity you gave us.

Victoria Goes to Brazil copyright © Frances Lincoln Limited 2009
Text and photographs copyright © Campos and Davis Photos 2009

First published in Great Britain and the USA in 2009 by
Frances Lincoln Children's Books, 4 Torriano Mews,
Torriano Avenue, London NW5 2RZ
www.franceslincoln.com

Acknowledgements
The author wishes to thank Grandfather, Vovô Luís & family; Grandmother, Vovó Maria & family;
Cecília Scodeller de Campos; Edgar & family; Sr Pedro; Maria Antônia & family;
Joyce & Mayumi; Aunty Florentina & family; Isaque & family; Raquel & Raquelle; Célia & Roger;
Maeve & family; Uncle José & family; Esther & family; Igrinalva & family; Fafá & Isadora;
Sr Daniel Fresnot & Casa Taiguara; Dona Yone e Dr José; Érica & Rodrigo; Escola Caminhando;
Grupo de Capoeira Abadá; EMATER; IAPAR; Sr Élcio; Sr Ildefonso; Sr Hugo Vidal;
Sr Sérgio Schimit; Sr Zampieri; & Sr Paulo Cristóforo & family for all their help.

British Library Cataloguing in Publication Data available on request

ISBN: 978-1-84507-927-7

Printed in China

1 3 5 7 9 8 6 4 2

Victoria
Goes to Brazil

Maria de Fatima Campos

F

FRANCES LINCOLN
CHILDREN'S BOOKS

North Atlantic
Ocean

BRAZIL

PARANÁ STATE

Campinas

Londrina

Itu   SÃO PAULO

Tamarana

Curitiba   Ilha Bella

Paranaguá

South Atlantic
Ocean

BRAZIL

The school holidays are nearly here! Mum is busy getting our travel documents ready, because she is taking me to Brazil, the country where she was born.

She has given me a book for drawing and sticking in pictures to show Dad and our friends when I come home.

São Paulo

We arrived early in the morning at Guarulhos Airport in São Paulo. This is the biggest city in South America and it was very busy, with planes arriving all the time.

I was very tired, but over the moon at the thought of meeting my Brazilian family!

Maria Antônia (I call her "Vovó Nensa"), Mum's best friend, was waiting for us with her daughter Alessandra and son-in-law Márcio. They spoke to me in Portuguese, the main language of Brazil: *"Seja Bem Vinda!"* ("Welcome, Victoria!") and gave me a big hug and kiss. Their dog Lua gave me a kiss too.

Then Vovó Nensa drove us to the car ferry.

I was hungry, so we stopped for lunch in a farm restaurant. Vovó Nensa ate *feijoada* – a pork dish invented by Africans who came as slaves to Brazil a long time ago.

We took the ferry to Ilha Bella ("Beautiful Island") where Vovó Nensa lives. It was very busy with cars coming and going, and people selling things.

We arrived in the evening at Vovó Nensa's house and I went straight to sleep!

Next morning, Vovó Nensa let me help make watermelon juice for breakfast with lemon juice and water. Vovó Nensa turned on the liquidiser and in a few seconds it was ready. The juice was delicious.

Vovó Nensa and I went out to see the fishing boats arriving, and a fisherman showed us two big fish he had just caught. "You are lucky," Vovó Nensa said to me. "The sun is shining for you today!"

Mum took photographs of the sea, a church and some old buildings for me to stick in my book.

Aunty Joyce and my cousin Mayumi have come to spend a few days with us. Mayumi is half-Brazilian and half-Japanese. We had fun playing in the sand.

I wanted to go swimming in the sea. Mum said it was too cold, but I put on my swimsuit anyway. I dipped my toe in the water, and Mum was right – it was freezing!

Later we went to see how native Brazilian Indian people used to make *farinha de mandioca* (casava flour). Nowadays it is made with big machines, but you can still see people making it the old way.

Today we drove to Campinas to see Aunty Florentina, her daughter Vera and granddaughter Amanda. Aunty Flo was my grandmother's best friend, and she told me stories of their adventures together when they were children.

Vera has just bought a *chácara* (small farm) nearby and we
went there. It was surrounded by fruit trees, with flowers,
big stones to climb on and exciting places to explore.

Amanda and I put bananas
out on a branch and lots of
little Mico monkeys came to
eat them.

Aunty Flo cooked beef,
beans, rice and salad for us.
Then we had bananas too!

We travelled to Curitiba by sleeping bus. I slept all the way.
Curitiba is the capital city of Paraná State. Mum's brother, Isaque,
collected us and we stayed in his house with Aunty Marlene.

I was feeling so happy when
we went to see Vovô Luís, my
great-grandfather, and his
family. Mum used to spend
her school holidays with him
and my grandmother long ago.

Mum's friend Maeve took me to Rua das Flores ("Street of Flowers") to look at the paintings and street performers. I liked this artist's work. He did a fish drawing and gave it to me. Wasn't he nice!

Then we watched a festival of *capoeira,* a sport with dancers, *berimbau* and drums. They let me join in!

Today Maeve drove us to the port of Paranaguá to see a procession for *Nossa Senhora do Rocio* ("Our Lady of Dew"), the patron saint of Paraná. The saint's statue has a blue cloak one hundred metres long so that everyone can touch it while they sing and pray.

Maeve's sister Verediana, who is an English teacher, asked Mum if I could spend the afternoon with her class. I had a great time being a teacher and speaking to the children in English!

Uncle Edgar, who is a pilot, flew us to Londrina in his own little plane. It was so exciting! I could see the hills, the animals, the houses – everything – from up in the air. Uncle Edgar showed me how to be a pilot, too.

Here we are, landing in Londrina ("Little London").
The city was founded by English people a long
time ago.

Tamarana

Uncle Edgar drove us to Tamarana, the small village where Mum was born. We stayed at Great-Uncle José's farmhouse.

I woke up early and sat out on the back verandah. The birds were singing – and suddenly I saw two green *piriquitos* in a tree, eating bananas!

After breakfast I went with
my cousins Rafaela and Mateus
to feed the chickens.

Then we all looked at the photos
and books that Mum and I
had brought from London.

Later we went to see my
great-grandmother Maria.
She is a Brazilian Indian from
the Tupi-Guarani Tribe in
southern Brazil. She gave me
a big kiss!

 # Londrina

When we got back to Londrina, I stayed at Aunty Igrinalva's house. We went out fishing with my cousin Márcio and his daughter Sofia.

The next day we went to the park. Sofia and I wanted to see the *capivaras* that live near the river. They looked like giant guinea-pigs!

Mummy wanted to show me how coffee grows, so we went to a coffee farm. The farmers were picking coffee beans and I helped them.

I also helped to move the coffee beans around so that they could dry evenly. I felt very grown-up!

Travelling back to São Paulo, we stayed with Mum's friend Fafá. We spent a morning in the Casa Taiguára shelter where lots of street children live. Mum says some of the big Brazilian cities have many children with nowhere to live. She and Dad have been helping the shelter since it opened.

As a special treat, Fafá took me to the local market. She knows how much I love drinking coconut juice and eating *pastel* – (pastry filled with cheese, chicken or vegetables).

The next day we went to Itu. Everything in Itu is BIG. I bought a BIG pencil for Dad because I was missing him, and when I'd finished my BIG ice lolly, I phoned him on the BIG telephone.

My last day in Brazil!

So many people came to see us that I had to write all their names down! The house was full of loud music and people were coming and going all day. My aunts did the cooking and my uncles got the barbecue ready.

This is me with some of my big Brazilian family. And this is where my story ends, because we are leaving tomorrow. I shall be sad to say goodbye, but Mum says we'll be coming back to Brazil soon!

Pastel Caipira cooked for Victoria

Serves 5 (about 20 pasties)

You'll need:

◆ **500g (2 ¼ cups) flour**

◆ **1 pinch of salt**

◆ **1 egg**

◆ **3 tablespoons vegetable oil**

◆ **150ml (1/2 cup) warm water**

◆ **500ml (2 cups) vegetable oil for deep frying**

◆ **Filling (suggested fillings: cooked beef with peas, ham and cheese, chicken with mushroom or leek, cheese and tomatoes with oregano, banana with honey and cinnamon)**

✛ a grown-up on hand to help you with the frying.

1. Put flour and salt in a mixing bowl, add 3 tablespoons oil and mix until the oil is absorbed.

2. Add the egg and mix again, then slowly add warm water to make a paste.

3. Knead the pastry for 10 minutes, then leave to rest for one hour.

4. Flatten the pastry with a rolling pin until it is very thin.

5. Put a tablespoon of filling on the pastry, then cut round it leaving about 3 inches (8cm) of pastry all the way round. Cover the filling by pulling edges of pastry together and press with a fork to seal. Do the same with all the pastry.

6. Ask a grown-up to heat 500 ml (2 cups) oil in a saucepan until very hot, then reduce to medium heat. Deep fry the pastel until it is pale golden, then remove and drain on a paper towel.

7. Eat it while it's hot!

Glossary

berimbau: one-stringed instrument made from wood and gourd fruit, used to accompany capoeira.

capivara: the largest living rodent in the world, related to the guinea-pig.

capoeira: a ritualised dance and form of self-defence created by African slaves who were sent to Brazil.

chácara: a small farm.

farinha de mandioca: casava flour.

feijoada: pork stew cooked with black beans and served with rice, casava flour, greens and oranges. It was invented by African slaves who used up the left-over bits of the pig such as ears, snout, tail and feet. It is the national dish of Brazil.

pastel: pastry parcel filled with savoury or sweet fillings and deep fried.

Seja bem vinda: You are welcome.

 Index

African people 12, 21
animals 11, 12, 19, 24, 28

barbecue 32
birds 26, 27
boat 15, 28
book 9, 15, 27
Brazilian Indian people 17, 27
bus 20

English language 23
English people 25
family 9,11,12,16, 18, 20, 24,
    26, 27, 28, 32, 33
farm 12, 19, 20, 26, 29
fishing 15, 28
food 12, 14, 17, 19, 29, 31, 32
fruit 13, 14, 19

island 13
Japanese people 16

market 31
music 21

painting 21
plane 10, 24, 25
Portuguese language 11

saint 22
sport 21
street performers 21
street shelter 30
swimming 16

About Victoria

Victoria was born with Down's Syndrome, a genetic condition caused by a baby being born with three copies of chromosome 21 instead of two. People with Down's Syndrome usually share certain physical characteristics, but more importantly, each child inherits his or her own family's looks and traits. Although all children with Down's Syndrome will have learning difficulties, their abilities vary widely.

Find out more about Down's Syndrome online:
UK   www.downs-syndrome.org.uk
USA   www.ndss.org   www.ndsccenter.org
Canada   www.cdss.ca
Australia   www.dsansw.org.au   www.dsav.asn.au   www.dsaq.org.au   www.actdsa.asn.au
www.downsyndrometasmania.org.au   www.dsawa.asn.au   www.downssa.asn.au   email: dsant@octa4.net.au
New Zealand   www.nzdsa.org.nz
Brazil   www.sosdown.com   www.ssd.org.br